Charles Ives
Take Me Home

Jessica Dickey

A SAMUEL FRENCH ACTING EDITION

SAMUEL FRENCH
FOUNDED 1830

SAMUELFRENCH.COM
SAMUELFRENCH-LONDON.CO.UK

CHARLES IVES TAKE ME HOME was produced at Rattlestick Playwrights Theater in New York City on May 29, 2013. The performance was directed by Daniella Topol, with sets by Andromache Chalfant, costumes by Michael Krass, lighting by Austin Smith, and sound by Broken Chord. The Production Manager was Eugenia Furneaux, and the Production Stage Manager was Kate Croasdale. The cast was as follows:

CHARLES IVES . . . . Henry Stram

COACH LAURA STARR. . . . . Kate Nowlin

JOHN STARR. . . . . .Drew McVety

CHARACTERS

CHARLES IVES – The modernist composer. Well into the latest years of his life, but full of enthusiasm and mischief and humor. Deeply subversive and humanist.

COACH LAURA STARR – 30s. Slightly butch, geeky, high school basketball coach. Takes the game very seriously. Great dribbling skills. Tough and vulnerable.

JOHN STARR – 50s. A talented violinist. Strict, patriarchal, devoted to his music, a cold father. Resentful of sports.

SETTING

The recent past. The set should be a simple, open playing area. Very sparse and intimate. An *Our Town* feeling.

THE MUSIC

All of the songs played by John on his violin are by Charles Ives. It may also be useful to be able to play a few moments of the Bach Chicon. The final piece of music that John plays, accompanied by Coach Starr, should be composed of the sounds and rhythms found in the play.

AUTHOR'S NOTES

The scenes in the play should ebb and flow like a piece of music, and there are moments of "rest" indicated. This should feel like a caesura in the action, like a leaf landing before the wind picks it up again. The play itself should feel like a piece of music. Ives himself loved to use dissonance in his music, often setting sharply contrasting tones and sounds next to each other. Let this give you courage in the staging and interpretation of the interplay of these three characters.

SPECIAL THANKS

Daniella Topol, Kate Navin and Gersh, David Van Asselt, Brian Long, Daniel Talbott, Denis Butkus, Julie Kline, the entire Rattlestick gang, Kate Croasdale, Diane Hassan and the Danbury Museum, Professor Roye Wates, Henry Stram, Kate Nowlin, Drew McVety, City Theatre, Tracy Brigden, Carlyn Aquiline, Keira Fromm, Strawdog, Curious Theatre Company, The New Harmony Project, Sewanee Writers Conference, the Lark, Morgan Jenness, Leah Hamos, the entire Dickey/Neff family.

*(A bare, simple space. **CHARLES IVES** enters while the house lights are still on. He is an older gentleman dressed in an old suit. Mischievous, bright, enthusiastic – a deep Musical genius. He addresses the audience.)*

CHARLES IVES. *(cheerfully)*

Hello everyone!

Hi hi hi!

(As the stage lights turn on –)

Oh!

(to the tech booth:)

Thank you.

(back to the audience:)

Welcome!

Thank you for being here.

Just a few things before we begin… Let's see…

Thank you for silencing your technological devices.

DO IT.

Thank you for not taking any pictures.

Thank you for not needing the bathroom.

And in the case of an emergency,

Thank you for running to the Exit that's back there.

Thank you for kindly tolerating whatever distractions your neighbor might cause.

You may also now thank your neighbor for tolerating you –

your elbows, your pocketbook on the floor (the fashion ever larger),

your emotional life, your fatigue.

Go on. Thank them.

(He waits until the audience has thanked each other –)

Good job.
Thank you for coming.
For using your presence as a vote, if you will,
That before we are all dead in the ground,
being in a room together is valuable.
I won't say important – there's no need to be ridiculous
– but valuable.

Thank you for learning all your lines.
No wait, that's me.

(He chuckles gently at himself.)

Thank you for chuckling at any and all tacit attempts
at comedy.

(More serious now – with great love)

Thank you for your comedy.
For the great folly that you are.
For your hypocrisy and emptiness and pettiness and
loneliness.
For your mortality, your loins.
All these will help you understand
The THREE HOURS traffic of our stage.

HA! I'm just kidding.
This'll be more like 75 minutes.

So let us begin!
Now in music, some say one begins with a "tune."
But for me, music always begins with a Sound.

(COACH STARR *starts dribbling. He listens, like it's a precious new language)*

And we're off – like a herd of blue turtles!

(COACH STARR *enters.)*

This is Laura Starr,
Coach of the Jerome High School Girls Basketball
team.

(**COACH STARR** *re-tucks her polo shirt into her pleat-front khakis. She stands before her team, in front of a chalkboard. She was never a cool person. She wears a gold chain that is too thick. Her pants are ridiculous. It is half time.*)

Coach Laura Starr was born during an unusually violent thunderstorm in April.

This may or may not relate to the fact

that she kicked her mother's tail bone on the way out and broke it.

COACH STARR.

Have a seat.

Get some water.

CHARLES IVES.

As she grew, her teeth came in prematurely,

so that by the age of one she had ten little baby teeth in her little baby mouth,

which made her look like a hairless baby LION.

Not mature enough to handle all those teeth, she was what you'd call a "Biter."

COACH STARR.

No talking, please.

Let's use – Private voices.

As in – Silence.

Let's just sit in silence for a minute and contemplate the first half of this game.

CHARLES IVES.

She was also a "Mover"!

From the time she could walk she had excellent coordination and showed an excelled proclivity for athletics.

COACH STARR.

And I'd like us to be honest.

I'd like us to be deeply candid

That the last 16 minutes on that game clock

Were not our proudest.
And it matters.
I would like us to sit here
On these Jerome High School locker room benches
And be unabashedly truthful –
In this conversation about the last 16 minutes (wherein
only I will speak)
That the first half of this game
And how we performed in the first half of this game
Matters.

CHARLES IVES.

The principal of Jerome High School had been
meaning to start a girls basketball program,
In part to address Title IX
(An item on the administrative To-Do list since its
inception in 1972),
But also with the hope of reducing the rising number
of teen pregnancies.
Surely young women would be less interested in
unprotected sex if they could do a lay-up.

COACH STARR.

Marieke –

Kimmy stands on the red line which demarcates the
boundary of our cherished sport – The referee hands
her the ball (As many referees have handed many
female players the ball –

A privilege earned in 1892 thank you very much Smith
College –)

And she throws that ball to you and you begin to
dribble,

And I swear to God, Marieke,

I swear to the Big Coach in the sky,

You look like a retard giraffe.

(She demonstrates.)

A retard giraffe
Shalloffaling down the court.

(She demonstrates.)

And it *matters.*

Ladies, we have been practicing 90 minutes a day
for the last 49 days in preparation for our first game
together,
And this is NOT what we practiced.

When they run a 2-1-2 defense –

You need to bump up the passing game.
You PASS until you find that hole and charge the lane
–

Either drawing two defenders so you free up the guard
to pop off a shot,
Or you can go for the lay up and draw the foul.

In our own defensive game you need to
USE your *KNEES.*
You need to hit the deck

(She slaps the floor, demonstrates.)

Butt DOWN,
Feet moving,
Palms UP.
USE those KNEES to SLIDE with your opponent –

(She demonstrates.)

Denise.
THIS is not defense.

(She demonstrates.)

Watch her WAIST:
Her feet will fool you, her arms will fool you –
But her WAIST will tell you exactly where she's going,
And your KNEES will take you there.
You've worked hard for those basketball knees, ladies,
so use 'em.

(She draws.)

There is a normal knee. Right? Yes?

(She draws.)

And then there is a basketball knee.
THEN –

(She pulls up her pant leg.)

There is a basketball knee.
It is a thing of horror –
But to devote your body to a task so much that the shape of the body changes –
That is a noble thing.
Does it look good in a – uh – lycra mini skirt?
Not a flippin' chance.
Does it make good defense?
You bet your mullet.
And it *matters.*

Ladies
You gotta DIVE for the BALL.
Dive for the ball more than seems reasonable.
Play the GAME
UNREASONABLY.
That's what we're here to do.
THAT is the ART.

*(We hear a violin. **JOHN,** middle-aged, worn out shirt with sleeves rolled up, enters.)*

CHARLES IVES.

Ah – and here comes John, once a student of mine.
Now the Concert Master and first chair of the Queens Symphony Orchestra in New York City.

*(**JOHN** enters.)*

Here we are John.

JOHN.

Here we are.

CHARLES IVES.

John Michael Starr was born in Kearnsey, Indiana.

His father brought a baseball glove to the hospital to welcome baby John.

(*JOHN gently moves the bow over the instrument, warming up. He is devoted to his instrument, and this has shaped his body, his manner.*)

The first year of his life John couldn't hear very well. So at the age of two he had surgery to help his little ears drain fluid...

(*JOHN gently moves the bow over the instrument, warming up.* **CHARLES IVES** *continues over the music.*)

His father Michael had been a gym teacher at the local high school,
But his mother Katherine taught piano.
John grew up the beneficiary of such musicianship in the home and quickly distinguished himself as having extraordinary promise.

(*JOHN looks up and begins to formally play his violin. He stops.*)

JOHN.
I went to Juilliard.

(*He goes to play again, but before he does – *)

I don't mind telling you that that feels good to say.
Like a sheriff showing his badge.

(*He goes to play something else, but stops – *)

This is fun.
It's like you're my Crowd.
I've always wanted to have a Crowd.

(*He plays, he stops.*)

I like TITS.
BIG.
The weirder the nipples the better.

(*He plays. Then stops – *)

Having a daughter is very confusing for a man.
(Women you should be aware of this.)
We spend our lives trying to touch the tits.
To lick them, rub ourselves on them.
And then we do
and a baby gets made
and the baby grows up to have tits of her own.
It's very upsetting.

(**JOHN** *whips off a gorgeous riff, bow high in the air.*)

That's just something Very Cool

that I can do.

I try not to speak and play at the same time.
It's wrong.
It's like – chewing gum while you sing,
or praying while you shit.

(*He goes to play, then suddenly remembers – *)

Actually, I did that once.
I was twenty, studying at Juilliard, when my mother
called.
My father had died.
I started the conversation in my pathetic little
kitchenette on 48th and 10th,
Where the sound of running engines was the
permanent accompaniment,
And somehow, by the time we hung up,
I was sitting on the toilet.

I put the phone on the sink
And started to…

He had a heart attack in the middle of the night.
In the kitchen.
He must've been searching for a turkey sandwich (he
did that).

They found him the morning, lying in front of the
sink.
Like a corn stalk after its been cut.

(Beat. He touches his chest.)

My father was the opposite of music:
Dirt that is pale on top.
Like this:

*(He drags his bow on the strings, ponticello. It sounds
like rust, dry leaves, tears.)*

Music is wet and pungent.

It leaves a stain.

(He plays something wet and pungent. **COACH STARR**
back with her team.)

COACH STARR.
They're walkin' all over our zone,
So second half we're gonna go man-to-man.
When you see a pick coming, let each other know, you
gotta talk out there.
And I wanna see you SWEAT.
Lemme tell you a secret ladies –
SWEAT is liquid GOLD.
Whatever HURTS in your life, whatever NEEDS
IMPROVED in your life – SWEAT will HEAL.
Effort. Sex. Need. Fear.
Anything that makes you SWEAT means the REAL
YOU
Is present.

(Then **LAURA**, *age 5, wet from a sweaty sleep. A kind of
strange stand off between her and* **JOHN**, *tender, filled
with effort, sex, need and fear.)*

JOHN.
You're all wet.

LAURA.
My room is hot.

JOHN.

I'm sorry.

I need an air conditioner.

I'm still getting settled.

(**LAURA** *just stands there, pajamas, sweaty, sleepy.*)

LAURA.

Is it cuz of me?

JOHN.

What do you mean?

LAURA.

Is cuz of me

That you live here now?

JOHN. *(heartbreak)*

No.

No no no.

It's not cuz of you.

…

It's just – your mom and I.

LAURA.

Didn't make it?

JOHN.

No.

LAURA.

Will we make it?

JOHN.

You and me?

Yes.

We'll make it.

Sweaty girl.

(*Back with her team*)

JOHN.

So there I was, twenty years old, my father buried in
the Midwest dirt,

when my teacher

William Schumann –

(He pauses in that academic way, to make sure you caught his name drop)

Told us that while he was away (doing some commission or other).
My idol would be teaching our class – composer Charles Ives.

It was just one class, but I was on the moon.

(CHARLES IVES *stands and prepares to teach class.)*

JOHN.

Charles Edward Ives was born in 1874 in Danbury Connecticut.
His father George banged the piano to imitate happy church bells
To announce that baby Charles had arrived.

CHARLES IVES.

Welcome welcome welcome! Hello good people!
Bill Schuman is a brilliant musician, and my friend;
I shall attempt to fill his very *laaaaaaaarge* shoes!

JOHN.

Pick up any piece of Charles Ives' music and you will hear
Dissonance, humor, complexity, beauty.

CHARLES IVES.

You look like a cluster of woodland creatures –
turtles, groundhogs, a porcupine!…
The twenties are very hard, aren't they?
Your childhood self no longer serves you.
But your adult self is still a distant shore.
And so there you TREAD.

(IVES mimes their tread)

JOHN.

He was fond of setting disparate styles against one another –
A ragtime with a requiem.

CHARLES IVES.

But old age is no better.

I don't mean to depress you,

(with a wink) – well maybe I do!–

But THIS is what you have to look forward to.

(IVES *sings an ominous first line of Beethoven's Fifth.)*

Your body cannot do what your whole life would wish it.

(sincerely, warmly)

But it's not all Bad, I promise.

JOHN.

He'd won the Pulitzer.

Given the prize money away.

His innovations literally ushered in the music of the twentieth century.

CHARLES IVES.

When I was a little younger than you,

I would sit in the town square and *listen* –

To the marching band rehearsing in the pavilion,

The choir practice coming from the Methodist Church,

And the high school football team practicing in the clover field.

All those sounds coming together in the air...

JOHN.

And here

He

was.

CHARLES IVES.

As a child I was always a little ashamed of music.

It felt silly to sit indoors and practice – all those LA LA LAs.

And maybe I wasn't wrong.

(a bit declarative)

Music as an art has been emasculated for far too long.

JOHN. *(earnest passion)*
YES. YES.

CHARLES IVES.
What is your name, son?

JOHN.
Me?
John. Sir. John Starr.

CHARLES IVES. *(checking his notes)*
John Starr…
I once knew a John Starr – fiddler of my father's band in Danbury – remarkable man.
And look at that- we have a private tutorial coming up later today, John Starr.

JOHN.
We do??!
YYYYEEAAAAHHHHH!!!

CHARLES IVES. *(happily startled by the loud sound)*
I do like your fervor, son.

JOHN.
Thank you sir.
I like your everything.

CHARLES IVES. *(kindly)* Alright then.

(**JOHN** *sits, honored, his hand on his chest*)

JOHN.
He called me "son"!

CHARLES IVES.
Now.
I want you to take out your textbooks, your scores,
Certainly anything by Debussy,
And I want you to take an enormous
POOOOOOOOH
Right on it.

I promised Bill I'd teach composition.
And I am a man of my word.

But just in case there is still an inch of your mind that
hasn't been decimated by the
TA TA TA that passes for music today,
I intend to make my case.

My young friends!
I say to you:
RUUUUUUUN FOR YOUR LIIIIIIIIIVES!

JOHN. *(whispered)*
(He was CRAZY.)

CHARLES IVES.
HEEEAAAAD FOR THE HIIIIILLLLS!

JOHN. *(whispered)*
(Totally CRAZY!)

CHARLES IVES.
What if I told you
That music has not existed before this moment!??

(JOHN *watches* **CHARLES IVES**, *mouth agape.)*

There is nothing to be taught!
There is nothing you need to know!
Your SOLE JOB
Is to strain with all your might
To hear that strange, clanging
Majesty
In your heart.
It will sound foreign to you, even *ugly...*
Do not
be afraid!

Listen.
Listen...!

(CHARLES IVES *refers to their hearts beating in their*
chests.)

What do you hear in there?

(He waits in silence while the class tries to listen to their
hearts.)

How will you ever know
If you're too busy with the
TA TA TA?

JOHN.
Charles Ives had also lost his father at age twenty.
Pivotal moment of his life.

CHARLES IVES.
What if the birth of music, of all art, will take place
When the last man who wants to make a living off of
art
Is gone forever?

JOHN.
With mine in the ground only months before,
I looked at Charles Ives as a kind of New Father,
(However crazy)–

CHARLES IVES.
What if there is only you
And the cacophony of your soul?
What would you play then?

JOHN.
– One that might lead me Home.

(beat)

CHARLES IVES. *(like a sneaky elf)*
Do you like
SPORTS?

JOHN.
And then he spent the next 45 minutes talking about
SPORTS.

(COACH STARR, *age ten, dribbles in – she weaves* *around* **JOHN** *and* **CHARLES IVES. COACH STARR** *dribbles spiritedly, narrating her fantasy superstar* *game.)*

COACH STARR. *(as the sports announcer, dribbling)*
Last ten seconds of the championship.
Laura Starr makes her way down the court…

JOHN.

Laura – ?

What are you doing here?

COACH STARR.

Boy is she really on her game tonight –

(She comes close to knocking his instrument.)

JOHN.

(Hey watch the violin!)

COACHSTARR.

FIVE – She throws off one opponent –

JOHN.

Laura it's not my weekend.

COACH STARR. *(still narrating her fantasy game)*

FOUR – She throws off another –

THREE – Look at that spin move!

Let's see that in slow motion –

JOHN.

I have a MAJOR audition today.

MAJOR

COACH STARR. *(slow motion voice as she repeats the spin move)*

Oooooh Mmmyyyyyy Gggoooooood –

JOHN.

LAURA!

*(Her fantasy game abruptly ends. **CHARLES IVES** looks on.)*

COACH STARR.

Dad! I was about to win the championship.

JOHN.

LAURA! Are you hearing me?

Answer me when I am talking to you.

COACH STARR.

WHAT.

JOHN.

This audition is MAJOR.

It's for the Frankfurt Symphony Orchestra!

Do you know what that means? – We're talking Dream Job! – MAJOR!

COACH STARR.

Frankfurt? Where's that?

JOHN.

Well Frankfurt is in Germany.

But the audition is in midtown and I am leaving in five minutes.

COACH STARR.

Germany? Cool.

Maybe we could have a backyard with a basketball hoop.

JOHN.

– Well – Laura – I don't think –

I don't know how it would work – with your mother – I don't –

I have to get the job first. Which means I have to nail the audition.

You know what I'm saying?

COACH STARR.

Okay. Can I help?

JOHN.

Okay you wanna help me? Wanna know how you can help me?

You can cross every single finger and arm and leg you have.

I need you to CROSS EVERYTHING.

Can you do that?

COACH STARR. (*jock swagger*)

Yeah

JOHN.
Lemme see.

(*While she crosses her arms and legs and fingers he manages to finish packing up for his audition.*)

Oh wow, very good, that is definitely gonna help me NAIL IT.
So now – wait a minute – how did you get here?

COACH STARR.
I walked. Well, I dribbled.

JOHN.
Across the park!?!? Jesus Christ you are ten years old you can't just walk across the park it's far too dangerous
Does your mother know you're here?

COACH STARR.
(I'm strong you know it's not that far.)

COACH STARR.
She locked me out.

JOHN.
She what?

COACH STARR.
She locked me out.

JOHN.
What do you mean she locked you out?

COACH STARR.
She said if I used that kind of language I wasn't welcome in her house.

JOHN.
What language?

COACH STARR.
Asshole.

JOHN.
Where did you learn the word asshole?

COACH STARR.

You. Every time you get a letter from the New York Philharmonic

You say that they can lick your asshole.

JOHN.

Touché.

COACH STARR.

So she locked me out and I came here.

(Well not right away at first I pounded on the door and rang the doorbell a hundred times and screamed asshole at the top of my lungs but then I came here.)

JOHN.

Jesus Christ

COACH STARR.

You know how she is!

JOHN.

Look I don't know what you and your mother have going on but this is not a good time, okay?

COACH STARR.

But can't you say something to her?

JOHN.

Like what Laura?

COACH STARR.

Like don't lock me out

JOHN.

Laura – I'm afraid I'm not going to be much help with your mother.

COACH STARR.

But –

JOHN.

No! You and your mother have to sort this out yourselves.

(She starts dribbling again)

JOHN.

Laura, stop that I have to go.

COACH STARR. *(still dribbling)*
Stop what?

JOHN.
That –

COACH STARR. *(still dribbling)*
That what?

JOHN.
That – bouncing –

(He tries to take the ball from her.)

COACH STARR.
The big ugly guy comes at her –

JOHN.
Stop it – Laura –

COACH STARR.
But she's too quick for him! –
How does this ten year old do it?!?!

JOHN.
Laura give me the ball.

COACH STARR.
She is DOMINATING her opponent.

(He really tries to get the ball.)

JOHN.
Laura – !

(He lunges at her, awkwardly succeeds in getting the ball, but clobbers her.)

COACH STARR. *(really hurt and really mad)*
Ow, Dad
That was a big-time foul!
A foul is when you push the player or slap their hand – you can't do that.
There are rules you know.
You can't foul people.

And you can't stay in middle lane here that's called Holding in the lane.

And if you're dribbling and you stopped and went to shoot and your feet lifted off the ground but

then they came back down and then you tried again that would be called Up and Down.

And if you knock it out of bounds it's called Out of Bounds.

JOHN.

These are very creative names.

COACH STARR.

Yeah, well…

JOHN.

We need to call your mom.

COACH STARR.

Why can't I just stay here?

JOHN.

Because

I'm leaving for this audition and I DON'T HAVE TIME.

COACH STARR.

…

JOHN.

Goddammit I'm sorry, Laura.

I'm sorry that things are the way they are.

I'm sorry that your mother is an asshole.

I'm sorry our marriage was a disaster.

I'm sorry that dreams fail.

I'm sorry that concessions are necessary.

I'm sorry

That I did

A FOUL

on you.

(She starts to leave.)

JOHN.

Where are you going?

You cannot walk across the goddamn park.

COACH STARR.

It's not that far go do Frankfurt.

(**JOHN** *grabs his hair, utterly stressed for a moment*)

JOHN.

FUCK! Alright I'll drop you at your mother's on my way I'll just be late.

COACH STARR.

I'll WALK IT OFF. Coach says when you get fouled to WALK IT OFF.

JOHN.

Well you walking back across that park would be a very bad foul.

COACH STARR.

Well then I guess we'll both have to WALK IT OFF.

(*She leaves and* **JOHN**'*s chest hurts. He looks at* **IVES** *for a moment, then goes to his seat.*)

COACH STARR.

We have a limited amount of time, right?

That's the game, right? – there is a set amount of time.

And you can't beat Time, ladies.

That Big Buzzer is a-comin' for ya.

And what is it saying when it delivers its faithful, terrible, gym-smellin' roar? –

(*She makes the loud, obnoxious sound of a gym buzzer.*)

TIME.

(*She makes another loud, obnoxious sound of a gym buzzer.*)

TIME is a-comin', ladies.

I know you think you're gonna be different.

Right now

Your bodies are tight.
Colagen.
Calcium.
Carried by bright, pulsing blood cells
Through your bright, pulsing blood.
When you touch your hips you feel bone.
When you put in a tampon – there's no moment of
"Oh boy,"
There's only "puhpt" – and in it goes.
The idea of lubricant embarrasses you.
But trust me, ladies.
It's coming.

Right now you have all this water –
A whole river of it – rushing through your entire body,
Pushing out of every hole in the tight soft bread of
your skin.
You cry every day – Or every other day –
Over something –
Derek Small hasn't called you back;
You saw him with Missy Helman and she's got bigger
tits.
The D on your Trig test.
Your fat legs.
Your favorite rock star.
Your Jordache jeans.
You cry over your life.

As you get older you don't necessarily cry less,
But there is not enough water, so it *costs*, rather than
relieves.
Your face, your hair – it's all drier.
And where does it go?
Where does all that water go?
Where all water goes, I guess.
Into the air.
That's what living is. That's where the toll is paid –

Every moment, with all its moisture, evaporates.
Is sucked into the space around us...

(She makes a sucking sound)

Which means it's still there...
The moment your father's father was born –

(Sucking sound)

Your parent's divorce –
Your fifteenth birthday –
The first half of this game –.

(Sucking sound)

And all you have, your sole possession,
Is your Devotion.
And your Devotion is already showing.

(She touches her brow)

If you've devoted to worry,
It will show here.

(She touches her spare tire.)

If you've devoted to television,
It will show here.

(She touches her knees)

If you've devoted to defense,
It will show here.

I know you don't think I know much.
I'm not cool.
I've got basketball knees,
I say "oh boy" when I put in a tampon,
I use lubricant.
And I *know*.
I KNOW – :
You

will

too.

JOHN. *(fierce)*

Frankfurt.

I nailed that goddamn audition.

I remember it perfectly – I played the Bach *Chicon* – I walked in there, rushed, upset, furious, and I played the SHIT OUT OF IT. And I GOT IT. I GOT FRANKFURT.

I would've moved to Europe and BEGUN – Frankfurt, then maybe London, Berlin.

But then I thought,

(JOHN *hears* **LAURA** *– dribble dribble dribble)*

I have a daughter.

(dribble dribble dribble)

I have a daughter.

(dribble dribble dribble)

I have a daughter.

I turned it down.

I turned Frankfurt down.

CHARLES IVES.

Do you regret that?

JOHN.

It seems like things should've turned out differently.

Why didn't it?

You chose family over music.

CHARLES IVES.

I chose family to GET to music.

I chose business to get to my family and my music.

I loved business!

A business negotiation – (especially a contentious one!) – is like a wonderful fugue!

Life insurance, Frankfurt, secretary, biologist.

It's like focusing on the notes and forgetting the song.

No *job* makes a happy life, John.

JOHN.

But what if your life – doesn't like you?

CHARLES IVES. *(poignantly)*

Well that would be a wonderful tragedy, now wouldn't it?

(Back to class)

All music is founded on repetition.

Take baseball for example!

> There are nine players on each team,
>
> And there are nine innings.
>
> Each inning consists of your team batting and my team fielding,
>
> And then my team batting and your team fielding.
>
> Pitch, hit, run, throw, OUT!
>
> Pitch, hit, run, throw, SAFE!
>
> It's the same song with subtle variations.

But if we could zoom out a bit – we'd hear the crowd cheering
The players sweating, the coaches screaming.
And if we zoomed out even farther out than that –
We might hear the park.
The northeast.
The Universe.

Music IS repetition.
Just like memory.
In fact, without memory there would be no music.
Think about it my little woodland creatures! –
As we listen to a piece of music we *remember* the tones we have just heard
And we *connect* them to the tones we are hearing.
This is memory.
That's why listening to music, if the music compels you to really *listen* – feels like coming Home.

(**COACH STARR**, *age 11, puts the medal around her neck.*)

COACH STARR.

I won!

Dad? I won!

(She holds up her medal.)

JOHN.

Whoah kiddo. It's Wednesday.

COACH STARR.

I won! See?

I won the free throw contest.

I made 21 out of 25.

I won.

JOHN.

21 out of 25, huh?

COACH STARR.

Yeah. I missed four.

But it was okay because everyone else missed more.

JOHN.

Come here.

LAURA.

– Why?

JOHN.

So I can see your medal.

(She crosses to him and stands near him.)

Your medal is very fancy.

COACH STARR.

I know. Do you have any music medals?

JOHN.

Uh, no. They don't uh they don't really give out medals in music.

COACH STARR.

Why not?

JOHN.

Because they uh – I don't know Laura, listen –

COACH STARR.

Well that's okay because I was thinking I could keep my medal here.

So. We can share it.

(She suddenly puts the medal around his neck. Totally surprised, he touches the medal, then hugs her. She hugs him back, her head down. Maybe it's a little awkward.)

COACH STARR.

(Ow.)

JOHN. *(gently, after they've parted –)*

I'm so touched.

Thank you. For sharing your medal with me.

COACH STARR.

My coach says if I do this summer camp at the Y my form will improve and I could be REALLY GOOD.

JOHN.

That's great. Come on I can take you home.

COACH STARR.

Mom's waiting in the car.

(He looks out the window, sees the car waiting.)

JOHN.

She is??

(He adjusts himself somehow, maybe his hair or something, as if she might see him.)

COACH STARR.

The deadline already passed but he said if I bring a check tomorrow I can still do it.

JOHN.

What deadline?

COACH STARR.

For the basketball camp. At the Y.

JOHN.

– ? – I don't understand.

COACH STARR.

My coach said if I bring a check –

JOHN.

Uh huh

COACH STARR.

I can still do the camp. At the Y.

JOHN.

…

You came here to ask for a check?

COACH STARR.

…

For camp so I can be really good.

JOHN.

I already sent your mother your money.

COACH STARR.

I know but it's only $190 and my coach said –

JOHN.

$190!?!?

COACH STARR.

It's a week.

JOHN.

$190?!! Jesus Christ! – Nothing at eleven years old should cost $190.

COACH STARR.

I wanna play basketball, Dad.

JOHN.

Can't you play basketball for free?

COACH STARR.

Not if I want to be really good.

JOHN.

Did your mother put you up to this?

COACH STARR.

She said you'd say no.

JOHN. (*looking out the window agian*)
Oh she did did she?
And what did her new boyfriend say?
what's his name – ?

Oh yes – *Chad.*
Sounds like a bad cologne –
Chad

COACH STARR.
Dad, you know his name Dad.

COACH STARR.
Mom only cares about being pretty.

JOHN.
Well there was a time when she cared about more than that.

COACH STARR.
Like when?

JOHN.
Like when we met. I was studying at Juilliard, and she worked at the little coffee shop across
Broadway there. She thought I was very fancy.
There was a time I hoped to be very fancy you know.

COACH STARR.
…

JOHN.
($190)

COACH STARR.
Didn't you pay for lessons to be really good?

JOHN.
No. My mother taught me –

COACH STARR.
Well nobody can teach me basketball and I want to be REALLY GOOD.
I wanna play basketball, Dad.

I wanna play basketball my WHOLE LIFE.

I wanna sleep in my sneakers.

I wanna do hand strengthening exercises in my sleep.

I wanna be 6 foot 9.

I wanna paint my room like a three second lane.

I wanna practice free throws in the shower.

I wanna POOP referee whistles!

(**CHARLES IVES** *has a good laugh at that one.* **JOHN** *glares at him, then back to* **COACH STARR**.)

JOHN.

$190.

COACH STARR.

Please Dad.

Please please please please please please please please.

Please Dad.

PLEASE PLEASE PLEASE PLEASE PLEASE PLEASE PLEASE PLEASE.

JOHN.

It's just tape on the ground and a basket in the air.

What is the point of basketball, Laura?

COACH STARR.

I don't know I just love it.

JOHN. *(under his breath)*

Yes, you and Charles Ives.

COACH STARR.

I love it I love it I love it I love it.

JOHN.	COACH STARR.
What can you do with basketball Laura?	
It's a fucking *game.* /	
(Don't say fucking –)	I fucking love it!
(Oh god.)	

(She's on the ground begging now.)

COACH STARR.

I love it I love it I love it I love it.

Please please please please.

(She starts to sing her begging to the famous cadence of Beethoven 5th)

PLEASE LET ME GO!
PLEASE LET ME GO!
PLEASE LET ME GO PLEASE LET ME GO PLEASE LET ME GO!

JOHN.

Oh Christ.

COACH STARR.

PLEASE LET ME GO PLEASE LET ME GO PLEASE LET ME GO!

(Her singing-begging continues. Very enthusiastically. She sways between singing and kissing her basketball like a lover. **JOHN** *looks at* **IVES**. *She is very entertaining.)*

JOHN.

Oh Jesus Mother of Christ– Very well.

COACH STARR. *(She stops.)*

Really?

JOHN.

Yes.

COACH STARR. *(top of her lungs)*

YYYYEEEEEAAAAAAHHHHH!!!

(She throws her arms around him, victorious.)

JOHN.

$190 for basketball.

(to **IVES***:)*

(Maybe it'll keep her from having sex.)

COACH STARR. *(a little quieter)*

Thank you, Dad.

Thank you for letting me go to the camp.

*(***JOHN*** gets out his checkbook and sits with great heaviness, writes the check. It is tense. Very quietly, she sings her thank yous – same Beethoven tune.)*

COACH STARR.

Thaa-aankyou, Dad. Thaa-aankyou, Dad.

Thank you Dad Thank you Dad Thank you Dad.

Thank you Dad Thank you Dad –

JOHN. *(cutting her off but pleased)*

Alright that's enough. Beethoven is turning in his grave.

(He hands her the check.)

Now get out of here.

And you tell your mother than MUSIC paid for your camp!

*(**COACH STARR** runs out.)*

CHARLES IVES.

Poop referee whistles!??

That was good.

JOHN.

I'd never seen her so happy in my goddamn life.

CHARLES IVES.

Making a child laugh is like sunshine in your ear.

Little Edith used to sit under my feet while I wrote,

And I would purposefully knock my shoes into her fat leg now and then

(Ever so gently, mind you)

Just to hear her laugh.

I tried to repeat that sound in music – couldn't be done.

Between you and me I stole that trick from my father.

I'd sit under our piano by the pedals and he would pretend to confuse my leg for the damper.

Oh I loved that!

JOHN.

The only time I ever saw my father happy was when he watched sports.

He would take me to the games and I just hated it.

I didn't understand the rules and everyone smelled
like bad cologne
And grown men would hug over the stupidest things –
A ball over a fence or a man outrunning another.
And yet my father was *mesmorized.*

I remember thinking –
What it would that be like?
For him to look at me with all that
Wide eyed
Adoring
Enthusiasm?
Rather than his usual
Dry lipped
Uncomprehending
Disdain…

He loved baseball best.

CHARLES IVES.
Baseball is a glorious sport.

JOHN. *(resentful)*
Well I couldn't play baseball.
Or football.
Or anything my father loved.
I practiced in the cellar so he wouldn't hear.

(**JOHN** *plays, then suddenly stops.*)

JOHN.
I feel – odd.
Like my chest is being pulled out my back.

CHARLES IVES.
Oh John, there isn't much time!

JOHN.
There isn't?

COACH STARR.
Ladies, this is our first game!
You gotta tap into that fire when you hit the court.

You gotta protect your most valuable possession!
What is your most valuable possession?
If you're me, you're thinkin' "this smokin' hot bod."
That's a joke.
It's the BALL.
The ball is your LIFE. Guard it as such.
See?

Your opponent knows this is your prized possession, so they'll try to take it.

(She demonstrates keeping the ball on your right hip when you dribble)

They want this *(the ball)*?
They gotta get through this *(the left arm),*
This *(the left hip)*
And this *(the rest of the body).*

Keep your legs wide, vary your tempo.
Keep them surprised.

*(***JOHN*** *tries to focus while* ***COACH STARR*** *dribbles with varying tempo – demonstrating.* ***JOHN****'s heart hurts.)*

JOHN.

Jesus Christ, at least be in time!

*(***COACH STARR*** *stands up, dribbling with steady tempo. This goes on until sadness is felt.)*

COACH STARR.

This rhythm, boring, where's the surprise?
WRONG.

JOHN.

Laura!

COACH STARR.

Then there's Marieke wrong.

(She demonstrates the retard giraffe.)

JOHN.

Laura!

(**COACH STARR**, *age 13, stops dribbling, takes a few steps toward* **JOHN**.)

COACH STARR

Yeah?

JOHN.

What have I said about dribbling while I practice?

COACH STARR.

Don't.

JOHN.

That's right.

COACH STARR.

But I gotta practice too.

JOHN.

Oh yeah?

COACH STARR.

Yeah.

JOHN.

Do you have a major audition coming up?

COACH STARR.

No.

JOHN.

Well I do, so that settles that.

COACH STARR.

What's it for?

JOHN.

…What?

COACH STARR.

The try-out. What's it for?

JOHN.

…The *audition* – is for the New York Philharmonic.

COACH STARR.

When is it?

JOHN.

When is what?

COACH STARR.

The *audition.* When is it?

JOHN.

Oh. Well. It's – coming.

Someday.

COACH STARR.

Coming someday?

Like for real? – or –

JOHN.

Laura.

Every performance of the Queens Symphony Orchestra is a potential audition for the New York Philharmonic.

(They look at one another for a moment – awkward stand-off.)

COACH STARR.

So can I dribble?

JOHN.

Laura. I'm sorry you didn't want to go to see the exhibit with me.

I thought that would be a nice activity for us.

COACH STARR.

Why do we always have to "do" something? I'm thirteen. We can just hang out.

JOHN.

Well this is me hanging out.

COACH STARR.

Well this is ME hanging out.

JOHN.

Okay. Since I am unable to practice over that racket, Would you like to learn some musical terms?

COACH STARR. *(pretends to consider it)*

Mmmm – NO.

JOHN.

I just thought since you are always making rhythm

At such a high volume,

You might enjoy knowing some musical terminology.

COACH STARR.

Is this a trick to make me join Band?

JOHN.

There is nothing wrong with Band.

I've made my life from Band.

COACH STARR.

Band kids are fat and mean.

JOHN.

Well as I recall, Jock kids are fat and mean.

COACH STARR.

NOT.

JOHN. *(new tactic)*

Laura, Music is an ART.

And as an Art, it requires Craft.

And Craft requires a series of techniques and symbols,
which when mastered and applied in an organized
way, make the Art. It's like cracking a code.

So listen, here are some of the techniques.

Pay attention.

Arco.

COACH STARR.

I don't want to do this.

JOHN.

I don't care. Arco.

COACH STARR.

Dad.

JOHN.

Laura. Please. When I DIE I would like to know that
I've left you with *something.*

So. Pay attention:

Arco is when you play with the bow.
Like this.

(He demonstrates.)

Arco.
Now you might slide between pitches, that's called
Glissando.

COACH STARR.

What? Glissero?

JOHN.

Glissando.
Glissero sounds like a prescription for erectile
dysfunction.

COACH STARR.

What's erectile dysfunction?

JOHN.

(Of course *that* you can say perfectly)
It's nothing – pay attention –
You might pluck the instrument, and that's called
Pizzicato.
See?

*(He plucks. **COACH STARR** uses the ball to imitate the
technique he's demonstrating.)*

COACH STARR.

This is what you're leaving me?

JOHN.

Or Col legno. See? – no hair, just the wood.
Tremolo.

(She dribbles to match the musical term.)

JOHN. *(growing irritated)*

Laura, pay attention – !

COACH STARR.

I am paying attention.

JOHN.

You're doing your bouncing again.

COACH STARR.

It's called DRIBBLING.

JOHN.

Well whatever, it's not a part of the musical lesson.

COACH STARR.

How do YOU know?!

(The tension builds as his irritation grows and he demonstrates this technique. He begins to play very loudly. As he demonstrates the "song" grows increasingly tense as he beats out the terms and **COACH STARR** *dribbles/plays along.)*

JOHN. *(plowing forward)*

Ponticello.

Double stop!

Fuguing!

Arpeggios!

Accelerando!

Crescendooooooo!

(He completes.)

JOHN.

FINISSIMO!

(They stare at one another, both incredibly hurt.)

That means we're finished.
Finissimo means finished.

(She continues staring at him. Hurt hurt hurt hurt hurt)

That means GET OUT.

CHARLES IVES.

Time out.
Let me be more helpful.

I cannot watch a sporting event without thinking of music.

Listen:

Time is the master of the body.

And the spirit is trapped inside it.

Just as the body must obey time, so must music.

(**JOHN** *quietly ghost plays, the wood on the strings, the list of terms while* **IVES** *speaks.*)

CHARLES IVES.

Music is written in the language Time –
4:4, 3:4, 6:8.
And yet the thing that does NOT obey Time –
Our divinity, our spirit –
Is trapped inside our instrument.

And so we labor relentlessly, painfully, with unending ache.
Through our instruments
Against Time.
And somehow through that struggle.
This divinity, this spirit, is liberated.
Tension – Release.
This is Music.

This is also sports!

JOHN.

Arco.
Glissando.

Pizzacato.
Col legno.

Tremolo. Ponticello.
Double stop.

Fuguing.
Arpeggios.
Accelerando.

Crescendo.

Finissimo.

(**COACH STARR** *demonstrates each referee's call with its appropriate hand signal*)

CHARLES IVES.

> Within the confines of Time, the Great Game Clock –
> The team groans forward, play by play, to the goal –
> The physical body fighting against itself and other bodies –
>
> To reach something that is utterly above the fray –
> A beautiful thing of achievement and metaphor.
>
> This trinity – the body, the spirit, and Time –
> Is the essence of life.
>
> *(Rest).*

COACH STARR.

> Charging.
>
> Traveling.
>
> Up and Down.
>
> Holding in the lane.
>
> Foul Tip Out of bounds Time out Time.

CHARLES IVES.

> John.
>
> *(An awkward silence between them.)*

JOHN.

> What?

CHARLES IVES.

> What are you thinking about?

JOHN.

> Music.

CHARLES IVES.

> Are you thinking about Laura?

JOHN.

> Laura?
> No.

CHARLES IVES.

> John.

JOHN.

> What?

CHARLES IVES.

Perhaps you ought to.

(Another awkward silence between them.)

JOHN.

Ought to – ?

CHARLES IVES.

Think about Laura.

*(**COACH STARR**, age 14, interrupts.)*

COACH STARR.

Charles Ives. worked in Insurance.

JOHN.

I beg your pardon?

COACH STARR.

He worked in Insurance. He was an Insurance Man.

JOHN.

How do you know that?

COACH STARR.

I read about him.

JOHN.

You read about him??

COACH STARR.

Yeah.

JOHN.

You went to the library

And picked up a book

And read about Charles Ives?

COACH STARR.

Yeah – which is how I know that he actually worked in
INSURANCE.

JOHN.

Laura – that's like the least important detail! He was an
AMAZING composer!

COACH STARR.

Well I listened to the Concord Sonata.

JOHN.

I'm sorry – (I feel lightheaded!) – You listened to *The Concord Sonata*??

COACH STARR.

Yeah. Not exactly CATCHY.

JOHN.

Laura, it's not supposed to be CATCHY.

COACH STARR.

Dad, chill out – I was hardly expecting The Indigo Girls.

JOHN.

– Meaning?

COACH STAR.

He's your favorite – so obviously I'm not gonna like it.

JOHN.

You don't know that. So what kind of music do you like? – these Indigo Girls?

COACH STARR.

They're awesome.

JOHN.

So what are they like?

COACH STARR.

Think lesbian harmony guitar poetry.

JOHN. *(disturbed on many levels)*

...

COACH STARR.

Exactly.

JOHN.

You might like Charles Ives. If you UNDERSTOOD it.

COACH STARR.

What is there to understand about Boring?

JOHN.

You know it's kind of amazing that you never met my father;

You open your mouth and its like his Jock Soul speaks from the grave.

I MET Charles Ives you know.

COACH STARR.

You met him?

JOHN.

True fact. My sophomore year at Juilliard

COACH STARR.

Holy shit.

JOHN.

That's exactly what I said.

I arrived for my tutorial

And there he was.

(**JOHN** *and* **CHARLES IVES**. *begin the tutorial. There is a tenderness between them.*)

CHARLES IVES. *(both then and now)*

He we are John.

JOHN.

Here we are.

Holy shit.

(**CHARLES IVES** *laughs.*)

IVES.

Let us begin.

JOHN.

What shall I play for you?

I know all your music! Or at least I'm going to! I went right after class and got a ton of it!

(**JOHN** *opens his bag and pulls out a huge stack of music.*)

CHARLES IVES. *(re: seeing all his music on the table)*
Oh Lord. It's like looking in the mirror and seeing your own rear end.

(They laugh.)

JOHN.
I'm sorry but can I just say something – ?
I love your music.
Your music opened up the world to me.
My class took a trip to New York City
And while everyone else went to a Broadway show,
I snuck off to hear whatever the New York Philharmonic was premiering.
It was your Second Symphony.
I had no idea music could be like that.
It was so deep and so – vast – it was about EVERYTHING –
And while I was listening something very strange happened to me –
I became aware of a pulse, kind of like a heart beat, and it said
"thank you
thank you
thank you"
over and over again –
Maybe it was the music itself, or maybe it just me –
But that's when I knew:
Music would be my life.

CHARLES IVES.
I don't know what to say. Thank you.

Alright porcupine! Let's have some fun, shall we?!

JOHN.
Yes! Alright!

CHARLES IVES.
Since we were talking about repetition earlier today (and it's right on top),

Let's start with "America."

This old chestnut!

I was no older than you when I wrote this.

(**JOHN** *gets out "America" and start playing,* **IVES** *accompanying.* **IVES** *suddenly breaks it off.*)

CHARLES IVES.

Oh Christ let's skip to measure 143 the interlude into the 5th Variation!

(**JOHN** *catches up.*)

Now – my father and I used to play this game – you keep playing

And see if you can guess what I'm playing!

JOHN. *(giddy)*

Okay!

(**IVES** *starts playing Violin Sonata #4.*)

JOHN.

I got it! I got it! – Sonata #4!

(**JOHN** *joins him on the Sonata.*)

CHARLES IVES.

Very good porcupine.

Here's another one!

(**IVES** *play the top of The Alcotts.*)

JOHN.

Oh that's easy! The Alcotts movement. Concord Sonata.

CHARLES IVES.

I wrote this for my daughter.

JOHN.

My turn – this is one of my favorites…

(**IVES** *keeps playing The Alcotts and* **JOHN** *starts playing "Things Our Fathers Loved."*)

CHARLES IVES.

Ah yes. Things Our Fathers Loved.

(**IVES** *joins* **JOHN** *on Things Our Fathers Loved. They play.*)

CHARLES IVES.

Okay stop. Let's start that one again –

JOHN.

Okay.

CHARLES IVES.

And let's see if we can make it more WET and PUNGENT.

JOHN.

– ? – Okay.

(*They start again. Then* **IVES** *stops him again.*)

CHARLES IVES.

Stop. You're technically excellent, but there's still too much Ta Ta Ta, can you feel that?

JOHN.

I don't know.

CHARLES IVES.

This is a song about lineage.

We are each a note on a deep primordial scale.

You are a note, your parents are a note.

And that scale

Goes

Up.

So there is a great longing in it, do you see?

Take it again. Just you.

Sit down, John.

(**JOHN** *tries again.* **IVES** *stops.*)

Tell me about your father, John.

JOHN.

My father?

CHARLES IVES.

This is a song about fathers, so tell me about yours.

JOHN.

…Well.

He died.

Two months ago.

CHARLES IVES.

…I see.

You know…

When you lose your father

The trees lean down.

JOHN.

The trees lean down?

What do you mean, how can trees lean down?

CHARLES IVES.

Have you not noticed?

It's like –

You look around, and see that

The trees are leaning down

Like they're sighing

Or giving up

Or listening

And at first it feels like sympathy,

Like the trees understand.

But then it starts to feel like…

Something else.

Something more –

Sinister.

Slowly

You recognize –

Like a high, hard string

Whirring its color blade into your brow–

It's not the trees at all.

The trees aren't leaning down.
The sky is closer.

(**JOHN** *touches his chest.*)

And *sky* isn't even the right word –
It's not *sky* like blue and clouds and youth –
It's more like – *the Universe* –
The cold, steel *Ether*
Is right there, *right there* –
Black and cold and Nothing – is right there.

The Universe is stretching out above you
And there is nothing there.
There is nothing there
Between the crown of your head
And that steel, vast
Shing
Of the Universe.

You lived between the afternoons.
You dreamed in greens.
Soaked the bottom of your pants in the rain.

But when your father dies, the sky goes with him.
And left bare is something entirely different.
Something permanent and frightening:
You
Are the top of that line.

(*They sit together quietly contemplating fatherlessness.*
Then **IVES** *stands.*)

Well John, I think we're done for now.
JOHN.
I thought of something – for my scale –
CHARLES IVES.
What is it?
JOHN.
My girlfriend.
She's pregnant.

CHARLES IVES.

Ah. Well then up you go.

(**JOHN** *starts to leave, hesitates.*)

JOHN.

I don't want to.

CHARLES IVES.

I know.

But John – the people we know in life

If we go about things the right way

Are like instruments we can pick up and play

Whenever we want.

Whenever we need.

You can come back to this at any time.

I'll be here.

(**JOHN** *nods.*)

Get Home safe now.

(**JOHN** *slowly makes his way back to the scene with*
LAURA.)

COACH STARR.

And that was me?

JOHN.

That was you.

He died. Not long after that.

(**COACH STARR** *doesn't know what to say.*)

COACH STARR.

Well that's cool that you knew him.

But don't you think it's significant that he was a musical
genius and he worked in Insurance?

JOHN.

Well it's very hard to make a living in music.

COACH STARR.

…?

JOHN.

So that's why he worked in Insurance.

COACH STARR.

That's not what he said.

JOHN.

Oh no?

COACH STARR.

No. Charles Ives loved this Thoreau quote:

"Instead of studying how to make it worth men's while to buy my baskets,

I studied rather how to avoid the necessity of selling them."

JOHN.

What is your point, Laura?

COACH STARR.

So that's why Charles Ives worked in Insurance.

He didn't want to make people buy his baskets.

JOHN.

And you're telling me this because –

COACH STARR.

Because maybe selling your baskets is what makes you so – mean. Or sad.

Maybe you should do something else for a living.

JOHN.

Something else for a living??

Music is my life.

Music is my joy, my deep.

Music is the only Home I have.

(A pained beat between them.)

JOHN. *(turning away from her, playing)*

Arco.

Glissando.

Pizzicato.

Col legno.

Tremolo.

COACH STARR.

I know the Symphony doesn't pay a lot.

JOHN. *(losing himself in the terms, shutting her out)*

Ponticello.

Double stop.

Fuguing.

Arpeggios.

Accelerando.

Crescendo.

Finissimo.

COACH STARR.

You're a dick.

(**COACH STARR** *back with her team.*)

COACH STARR. *(tenderly, sincerely, then it grows)*

It comes down to who you want to be.

You know what I'm saying ladies?

Who do you want to be?

And what are you waiting for?

I don't give a shit if you get married and have babies.

Or become some asshole's secretary.

Or a biologist over a petri dish.

Or a musician in Queens.

I'm telling you right now,

If you want a shot at being the best at that thing, whatever it is.

Then you have to dive for the ball right now.

No one is gonna GIVE you that ball.

You have to TAKE IT.

Teach yourself to TAKE that ball.

And if that ball is hard to get, and I bet it will be.

Teach yourself to DIVE for that ball.

Every ball, every day, every time. DIVE.

Dive dive dive dive.

DIVE DIVE DIVE DIVE.

DIVE –

(**COACH STARR,** *age 16*)

JOHN.

Oh shit, sorry I missed your game, we had our Valentine crap concert. I'll get the next one.

COACH STARR.

The season is over.

JOHN.

What?

COACH STARR.

It was the Championship.

That's why I invited you.

JOHN.

Oh. Sorry. How was it?

COACH STARR.

We won.

JOHN.

Nice.

Well, next year.

COACH STARR.

Sure.

JOHN.

Where's your stuff, it's our weekend, right?

COACH STARR.

Yeah, it's just that I have the SATs tomorrow, so…

JOHN.

The SATs, already?

COACH STARR.

Dad, Yeah, I'm applying to colleges.

JOHN.

Colleges? Jesus Christ I'm old.

COACH STARR.

Yeah, but um, I was thinking maybe you would wanna come with me to visit them.

JOHN.

Visit colleges? Um, sure, okay, you mean like now?

COACH STARR.

Um, no, not *now* per se – but I thought maybe we could do a road trip or something.

JOHN.

A road trip? Sure, road trip to where?

COACH STARR.

Um. Minneapolis.

St. Louis.

Um. Omaha.

JOHN.

Whoah whoah whoah The Midwest?

Are you joking?

COACH STARR.

You're from there right?

JOHN.

The Midwest??

The Midwest is where people are fat and mean and and and ignorant.

COACH STARR.

Well how am I supposed to know that without visiting?

JOHN.	**COACH STARR.**
Well I'm telling you now, you don't need to visit.	
	And what do you care?
What do I care?? Laura if you go to the Midwest then	
Every break or holiday you'll have to fly home	You went where you wanted
That's hundreds of dollars and I'll never see you	you went far away

	And you never see me now
Look I said I was sorry I missed	
The goddamn game	I don't care, I don't care if you missed the goddamn game you would've just sat there and scowled anyway

JOHN.

What do you want to go to the Midwest for?

COACH STARR.

Well, they have really good programs –

JOHN.

Programs for what?

COACH STARR.

Athletics. Their athletic departments –

JOHN.	**COACH STARR.**
Oh my god	
No no way	
It's time you started getting serious about your life.	
Instead of this basketball crap	I am serious about my life this is all very interesting coming from you.
(What does that mean Coming from me?) Do you think ATHLETICS	
Is actually a viable option I mean	Nothing nothing nevermind Dad Jesus
Jesus Laura I know right now you think it's fun But eventually you're going to be an adult	Christ just – nevermind.

And you will regret devoting
your life to a a a
Game, or a a a Passtime. I
mean what are you
Going to be with Athletics?
A a a – a what?

> A Coach.
> I will be a Coach.

Exactly. A coach? – Exactly.
No way. Not on my bill. No
    way.

    (Silence. It's bad. It's very bad.)

COACH STARR.
    Okay.

JOHN.
    …
    Okay? What is okay?
    LAURA??

    (**COACH STARR**, *back with her team*)

COACH STARR.
    – DIVE DIVE DIVE DIVE.

    (Her phonem suddenly rings. She pulls out a very large,
    Nokia mobile phone.)

COACH STARR. *(re: the large phone)*
    These things are really something, eh?
    Cellular mobile – birthday gift to myself this year.

    (She answers with swagger.)

    Hello Mother.
    I'm in the middle of halftime, can I call ya back?
    …
    Oh.
    When was this?

   ...

Oh wow. Okay.

   ...

Yeah.

   ...

No, no. I'm glad you –

...yeah.

Yeah...

   ...

Okay.

Yeah, I'll...

I'll call you after the game.

*(***COACH STARR***, age 17, can walk over to* **JOHN***'s violin. She touches it She sits. She tries to play it.)*

JOHN.

What are you doing?

COACH STARR.

Oh. I...

(She doesn't get up from the violin.)

JOHN.

Get up.

(She stares at the violin, trying to understand why he loves it so.)

COACH STARR.

   ...

JOHN.

Laura. Did you hear me? I said. Get up.

(Pause. When she doesn't, he walks over to her and snatches the bow and violin from her. She gets up.)

JOHN.

And where exactly have you been?

You haven't shown up for a visit in I don't know how long.

COACH STARR.

You could've called.

JOHN.

What?

COACH STARR.

When I didn't show up you could've called.

JOHN.

Is this a joke?

COACH STARR.

If you were so concerned about our visits why didn't you call?

JOHN.

Oh so it's my fault?

I should have called to MAKE YOU keep your scheduled visits, I see.

COACH STARR.

Just sayin'. You could have called.

JOHN.

No that's good to know, from now on I'll CONFIRM our visits like a fucking dental appointment.

Do you think they're gonna put up with that at SUNY Purchase?

COACH STARR.

I'm not going to SUNY Purchase.

(He blenches, totally caught off guard, half in the memory, half clutching his heart..)

JOHN.

What's happening?

COACH STARR.

I fly to St. Louis tomorrow.

I start training next week.

I wanted to –

JOHN.

St. Louis? Training? Training for what?

COACH STARR.

For the team Dad.

I'm gonna play basketball.

JOHN.

What?

COACH STARR.

I'm gonna play basketball.

JOHN.

Oh you are, are you, and how exactly do you propose
to pay for that?

COACH STARR.

I'm gonna play basketball, Dad.

JOHN.

Not on MY BILL you're not.

COACH STARR.

I got a full ride.

JOHN.

You what?

COACH STARR.

I got a full ride. The coach just called.

So it's not on "YOUR BILL."

I'm gonna play basketball, Dad.

(after a beat:)

JOHN.

Well, HAVE FUN.

COACH STARR.

I will.

JOHN.

(Oh god.)

COACH STARR.

I will have fun.

I'm gonna have so much fucking fun, Dad.

The fun is gonna be so overwhelming, you won't even
recognize me.

I'm gonna do suicide sprints.

I'm gonna lift weights 'til my tits shrink.

I'm gonna cut my hair short.

I'm gonna be mistaken for a guy at restaurants.

I'm gonna dress badly.

I'm gonna get tendonitis.

I'm gonna dream of three second lanes.

I'm gonna constantly have orange Gatorade tongue.

I'm gonna take Ibprofen every night.

I'm gonna become ambidextrous.

I'm gonna memorize offensive plays.

I'm gonna make foul shots with my eyes closed.

I'm gonna slide with my palms up.

I'm going to score.

And foul.

And charge.

And WIN.

And every FUCKING SECOND

Of all that FUCKING FUN

I am NEVER

NEVER

EVER

Going to think of

YOU.

(She goes back to the chalk board. **JOHN** *is in terrible pain, hand on his chest. He turns to* **CHARLES IVES**.*)*

JOHN. *(full on chest pains)*
What's happening?

CHARLES IVES.
Be calm.
Be still.

JOHN.
What's happening?
I don't understand.

CHARLES IVES.
John. I'm here.
I'm here.

(**JOHN** *looks the audience with sudden horror and suspicion.*)

JOHN. *(trying to get his footing like at the top of the play)*
I went to Juilliard.

(but he can't)

What's happening?!

CHARLES IVES.
John.
John.
Look at me.
Sit down.
Play something.

JOHN.
Play? I don't want to.

CHARLES IVES.
Sit down John.
Play.

(**JOHN** *hesitates.*)

Sit down, John.

(**JOHN** *sits to play.*)

Very good.
Just play.
And listen carefully.

(**JOHN** *plays.*)

You've had a heart attack.
Keep playing.
Your heart has given way.
And you are dying.
There is nothing to be afraid of.
There is nothing to be done.

You must simply play through.

(**JOHN** *stares at* **CHARLES IVES** *while he finishes the song.* **CHARLES IVES** *places his hand on* **JOHN**'s *shoulder.*)

Very good.

(**JOHN** *looks up and sees* **COACH LAURA STARR**.)

JOHN.
Laura.

CHARLES IVES.
Yes.
Coach Laura Starr.

JOHN.
Coach?

CHARLES IVES.
Yes. It's their first game.

(**JOHN** *and* **CHARLES IVES** *watch her speak.*)

COACH STARR.
Heart attack.
Who made that game plan, huh?
This idea – That a man,
Lives or dies by this soft pink fist in his chest.

(*She holds up her fist, makes it pump like a heart.*)

This
Decides when the game is over.
Or as my father would say, finissimo.

JOHN.
That's right. Finissimo.

COACH STARR. (*getting back on track*)
So let's go out there and KICK SOME PUSSY.
Kimmy, you lead the warm-up, get some water – run some lay-ups.
I'll be right out.

(She stops them before they leave.)

Before you go –
I want to thank you.

I know I'm very hard on you,
That I make you run a lot of sprints,
And particularly when "Aunt Flo" is in town
I can go crazy with the push-ups…
But I love our practices –
The squeak of your sneakers,
The smell of the gym floor…
It's just tape on the ground
And a basket in the air
But thank you for being here.
For knowing that being here has value –
I won't say it's important, or that it adds anything to
the world –
But it does have value.
To me.
And I hope it has value to you.
See you out there.

JOHN. *(taking her in)*
Coach Laura Starr.
It's easy when they're a baby.
But how do you love them when they grow up
And like sports and have tits
And hate you?

(**COACH STARR** *suddenly rises and begins dribbling.
She varies the pace and strength of her dribbling – She
demonstrates the musical terms.)*

COACH STARR.
Arco.
Glissando.
Pizzicato.

JOHN.
Look at her.
She knows all the terms.

COACH STARR.
Col legno.

(**JOHN** *joins her on his violin.*)

Tremolo.

(**COACH STARR** *dribbles tremolo, and* **JOHN** *plays it. Tremolo builds. Then suddenly she stops and puts the ball away.* **JOHN** *continues to play tremolo, not wanting it to be over. He slowly stops. An awful realization. He falls to his knees slowly.*)

JOHN. *(quietly, to* **LAURA***)*
No.

(to **IVES***)*
No.

CHARLES IVES. *(gently)*
I'm sorry John.

JOHN. *(quietly)*
Please.
Help me.
Please help me.

IVES. *(fatherly love)*
John.

JOHN.
I devoted my life.
I listened to your music
And it was – Vast
And deep
And Everything…

(Back to Laura:)

Why?
Why couldn't I see?

IVES. *(still with him, still loving)*
  Time John.

JOHN.
  Help me!
  I have nothing!

IVES.
  John.

JOHN.
  NOTHING!

  *(**IVES** goes to **JOHN**, who is on the ground, clutching his violin. **IVES** stands behind **JOHN**. Braces him.)*

IVES.
  John.

  Your sole job
  Is to strain with all your might
  To hear that strange, clanging
  Majesty
  In your heart.

  *(**IVES** holds his hands over **JOHN**'s heart.)*

  Listen.
  Listen.

  *(**JOHN** does.)*

  What do you hear in there?

JOHN. *(quietly, hearing his heart beat)*
  Thank you.
  Thank you.
  Thank you.

  *(**JOHN** opens his eyes, still holding his violin to his chest. He goes to her.)*

  Thank you, Laura.
  Thank you for the Valentine you made in the third grade.
  You wrote it on staff paper, my music paper,
  So I would like it, you said.

Thank you for sharing your medal with me.
Thank you for listening to the Concord Sonata
Even though you hated it.
Thank you for trying to explain sports to me
Even though I hated it.

Thank you
For hating me.
The guilt would've been worse if you hadn't.
And thank you for never saying it.
The hurt would've been unbearable if you had.

(**JOHN** *begins to see the future.* **IVES** *plays a few quiet bars of The Alcotts.*)

Thank you for hiring top notch musicians to play
At my funeral…:
The Concord Sonata, an excellent choice.
Thank you for keeping my violin.
Thank you for waking up
About a year and a half from now
And crying unabashedly in your bed for four hours,
Staring at the tree tops out the window,
Because you suddenly understand,
Like tripping over a floor board –
that your father is gone.
That
You
Are the top of that line.

CHARLES IVES.
Time, John.
John.
Time.

(**CHARLES IVES** *smiles and gently motions for the exit.* **JOHN** *rises, holding his violin, and exits.* **COACH STARR** *stands. She starts to dribble, narrating her fantasy superstar game, quiet at first, then growing.*)

COACH STARR. *(as the sports announcer)*
>Last ten seconds of the championship,
>Laura Starr makes her way down the court…
>The screams of the crowd all around her –
>After all these years she is finally at the top of her game.
>She throws off one opponent, she throws off another –

(The buzzer counting down.)

>Five! – she spins!
>Four! –
>SHE CHARGES THE LANE!!!
>THREE! – SHE SHOOTS!
>TWO! – Will she make it?
>**ONE** – !??! WILL LAURA STARR MAKE IT?!! –
>**SHE SCORES! LAURA STARR SCORES!**

(She continues the narration loudly, unabashedly:)

>**THE CROWD GOES ABSOLUTELY WILD!**
>**LAURA STARR HAS WON THE CHAMPIONSHIP**
>**OF THE WORLD!**

*(***COACH STARR*** *falls to her knees, her screams are both victorious and painful. Eventually, she composes herself, and exits the locker room.)*

*(**CHARLES IVES.** turns to the audience –)*

CHARLES IVES. *(with great love)*
>Well that concludes our evening together.
>Thank you again for joining us.
>Get Home safe now,
>Or wherever your travels take you.

FINISSIMO / END OF PLAY.

www.ingramcontent.com/pod-product-compliance
Lightning Source LLC
Chambersburg PA
CBHW070645120726

47909CB00004B/1590